Apostate
The First Heresy
C.J. Loveman

Breaking Light Press

Also by C.J. Loveman

Forthcoming Novel: *The Centurion's Embrace*
In the Works: *Protocol Heresy*

For those who were forced to choose between their faith and their self—and bravely chose both.

Chapter One

It happened on a steamy summer night, just after a church softball game.

The two came back to Calvin's place and needed a shower before dinner. Calvin held out the most luxurious towel in his linen closet, but they fumbled, both reaching for it, and Calvin landed one of his hands on the small of Kirk's back. His large palm enveloped the spot as Kirk lifted his upper body. Calvin allowed his hand to lower with gravity, and Kirk did nothing to remove it.

Their eyes met, each confessing their intense desire. As they pulled their bodies into a tight embrace, they finally felt the evidence of their pent-up passion. No longer playing games, they became engulfed in each other as their mouths joined and their hands explored.

Calvin would never, for the rest of his life, forget Kirk's scent, his taste.

Just when it seemed like they wouldn't be able to turn back, Kirk pushed back without warning and looked at the ground.

"No! I...I can't..."

Calvin was so disoriented from the sudden shift, it took him a moment to realize what it meant. Kirk gathered his things and started for the door while Calvin stood dumbfounded, at a loss for what to say or do.

Near the bus stop, propaganda posters were layered all around the old phone pole. The new images were slathered over the old in a protruding mass. A crimson background and large hands with the Church logo reached down to the masses with images of bounty, with "Meeting All Your Needs!" in large block letters at the bottom. It reminded him of a film series about the "end times" shown in churches decades earlier. The films had scared the hell out of people even as they'd tried to chase them into Heaven. Now, Calvin lived under the tyranny of theocracy, and the state-Church seemed content to hurl the entire world down the same dreadful path it had once feared.

On the edge of the poster, Calvin noticed a curious hole. He pushed at it with his fingertip, and soon his entire digit sank deep into the layers. Years of old paper and glue separated as if he were burrowing the depths for something precious. The approaching bus shined a spotlight on him, and he jerked his hand away and prepared his phone for scanning.

Calvin lumbered up the bus's stairs, a tote bag on his arm and his phone in hand. He glanced at the driver—in his peripheral vision, there was a young nurse in scrubs and an older man sleeping in his seat. He walked to the place farthest from the other two passengers and plopped down. A used newspaper lay sprawled across the seat next to him. He saw the headlines: "President Visits Tomorrow!" "Rioters at Church Headquarters Tied to Terrorists," and "U.S. Expands Sanctions Against Secular Nations." He tossed the paper onto the floor and stepped on it with both feet.

Calvin pulled out his prized possession: an antique Walkman from the 1980s. It had once belonged to his favorite uncle, so it felt like a family heirloom, but it also sheltered him from the endless propaganda. Rather than the radio, he would listen to his vast collection of cassette tapes.

Looking at the current rotation, he popped in "Eschatology Lectures, a Theological Study of the End Times," an old cassette by one-time prominent theologian Dr. Hulda M. Wyatt. How unsurprised she would be to see the world's current state. On the other hand, she would feel shocked and mortified to witness the Church's role in it all. The scenes whipping by the window didn't register in Calvin's mind because he had already wrapped himself in Dr. Wyatt's lecture; every passing moment increased his primal desire for sleep, and soon he even tuned out Dr. Wyatt.

Calvin disembarked, failing to avoid the message wrapped around the entire bus shelter: "Support the Government! Report to Church!" emblazoned in red with the happiest models on earth pictured in every open space. Pictures of the perfect Church-approved family. His instantaneous rage pulled him out of his slumber for a moment, and he turned off the lecture and began a ferocious internal rant as he walked toward the store.

A few days after Kirk had run out of his apartment, he called Calvin and asked to meet him at the church. They met on a Monday because the rest of the staff had taken the day off. Calvin walked in and saw Kirk pacing near the open sanctuary doors. His face looked pale, drained of the usual cheer that could brighten any room. His dark hair, always stylish and brushed forward, now hung unkempt like blinds over his eyes.

"Let's go talk in there," Kirk said, motioning to the pews in the back. They sat together.

Calvin knew to expect the worst, yet with Kirk's body heat so close, he couldn't stop his mind from wandering. He breathed deep, ingesting every particle in the air that they shared, archiving it deep inside.

"I don't know what happened at your place, but I almost quit over it," Kirk said.

"No! Why?" Calvin replied. "That seems a li—"

"But then I realized what happened was really about you, not me."

"What?" Calvin asked as he dropped his upper body back against the hard wood.

"Cal, you are gay or whatever, and misunderstood our friendship."

"Misunders—"

"You. You have to get yourself right, or one of us has to go," Kirk said.

For a moment, Calvin doubted himself. It was true that he had misread signals with friends in the past. But this time, he could point to direct contact, places, and ways that Kirk had touched him—all evidence from just a few days ago. He knew that the feelings were mutual, but he also felt desperate to salvage something between them. So rather than force Kirk to face his desires, he just accepted the blame.

"I'm sorry! I'm sorry! I'll do whatever you want. Please. Can't we still be friends?"

"Maybe, a long time from now, if you get yourself right."

"How lo—"

"I'll be praying for you, Cal," Kirk said.

He lifted his hand to hide the tears in his blue eyes and paused as if he had something more to say.

Calvin could feel the conflict raging inside him, but Kirk turned and ran out, leaving any of those words unsaid.

Calvin let out a primal scream. "Why?!"

Obscenities blasted out of his mouth toward the vaulted sanctuary roof. He felt tricked and betrayed. His whole life, he had lived only to serve, but now he was left alone with this mortal wound. Even as his anger toward life and God erupted from him, he wondered if he could ever be forgiven.

Chapter Two

The bank of ten monitors flickered a bluish hue across the cramped office. It hypnotized Calvin into a light sleep and then nudged him awake in endless cycles. This was the woeful reality of the life of a security guard—the only living thing in the store overnight.

He sent his hand across the particleboard desk and bumped into the radio. A classic country star yodeled after he turned it on, and Calvin's eyes lifted like two heavy garage doors just as the song ended. "This is a news brief from the Patriot & Prophet News Corporation—"

"Oh, god, bring back the yodeling!" Calvin said.

"God's Chosen, the President, on Wednesday detailed his plan to create a new international organization overseeing Church and morality initiati—"

Calvin's hand stung after he struck the radio with an open palm. He hit it so hard that the transmission turned off.

"It's all an abomination!"

Calvin tried to exhale his tension as he examined the radio.

After confirming that it still worked, he rose with the tightness of middle age and began his end-of-shift tour a few hours early.

In the stairwell, he steadied himself on the cold steel railing and descended to the store's lower level. The glistening white floor shone as he made his way to the exterior doors on the other side. He removed the scanner from his jacket and pointed it at a barcode on the door frame. It beeped, documenting his first stop.

A distant call came over a loudspeaker as he put the scanner back in his pocket. Pulsating police lights blinded him through the six glass doors; the colors grew more intense as they came closer. He couldn't help but wonder if they were coming for him.

You're paranoid, he thought.

"Stop!" the authorities yelled over their loudspeaker.

Calvin felt a brief moment of relief, knowing that they were hunting someone else.

"What the hell is going on out there?"

A man materialized from around the corner and crashed full-speed into the middle door. The impact released an explosion of glass, each shard colored by the approaching police lights. Calvin let out an instinctual scream, but was so transfixed by the scene, he didn't shield himself. The fresh-faced young man looked up at him in desperation.

Blood flowed down, covering the man's face, and he whispered, "Help. Please, help me," as he struggled to get up.

His voice sounded even younger than he looked. His bangs, now red, weighed down near his eyes.

Before Calvin could say or do anything, morality officers barged through the gaping hole. They wore their purple uniforms with crimson Church logos across their chests.

The young man was unable to stand; still, the officers tackled him and unleashed their rage. When they'd had their fill, they put the kid in restraints and put a hood over his head.

In only moments, the immaculate area looked and smelled like a slaughterhouse. Calvin, filled with disgust, wanted to beat the officers with the nearest blunt object.

"Stop! Are you planning to kill him right next to the children's department?"

One of the younger officers shot a death-stare back at him. "Mind yourself, rent-a-cop."

"Relax, officer." A svelte man in a black suit walked in, raising his hand.

Calvin noticed his slicked-back hair and the distinctive Church logo pinned to his lapel. "I'm Inspector White from Church Intelligence, and I'm sorry for what has hap—"

"Yeah! I've got a large hole where a door used to be. Glass and blood all over!"

"Copy that. But we have contractors on call. They will have this place cleaned and repaired in no time."

"OK, well, I'll have to write an incident report and leave a message for my supervisor," Calvin responded.

"Understandable. I will leave two officers behind to guard the door until everything is back to normal."

Calvin nodded as the officers moved the young man past him toward the door. The blood soaking through the hood made him nauseous.

"When The Righteous Judge gets through with you, you'll wish you died tonight," the younger officer told his prisoner.

Calvin bit his tongue as he turned around and made his way back to the security office. He spent the rest of his shift rewatching the security video.

"I don't know what they are anymore, but it's not a church!"

Chapter Three

Feeling emptied of everything inside, he stumbled to his church office and sat at his desk.

The next morning, Calvin woke with his senior pastor shaking him by the shoulders. "Calvin! Son, are you OK?"

Calvin looked up, feeling disoriented, and realized that his conversation with Kirk had not been a nightmare. He burst into tears as the weight of his sorrow covered him all over again. The head pastor walked him to his large office and eased him down onto the couch. Sitting next to him, he put his arm around Calvin and looked at him with a mix of bewilderment and genuine compassion. His facial expression changed after Calvin made an unsolicited but complete confession, telling his senior pastor that he was gay.

He sent Calvin back home and put him on administrative leave until a disciplinary committee reviewed the matter. Calvin, numb from pain, didn't react, but he knew what that really meant. He remembered his original calling into ministry: the supernatural vision he'd had as a preteen. It had supercharged him through his youth, the college years and even through most of his internal struggles. That calling served as his touchstone—a guide to navigate life, and a context for everything. He knew that his promising career and passion for ministry had died right there on his senior pastor's couch, and a fog of prophetic doom descended all around him. He knew it would be permanent.

The sun had just begun to pierce the sky when Calvin boarded the waiting bus. He made his way to the back and looked toward the store. Replaying the barbarism he'd witnessed earlier, he found himself admiring the young man. *I don't know what he did, but at least he did something.* The more he thought about the young man's voice, his build and face, the more he thought about Kirk. He wondered if Kirk had been swallowed whole by the Church—or had he eventually taken a stand for himself?

Calvin harbored hate for the state-Church, but had never taken concrete action. It seemed like a pattern through all the critical moments in his life, and he felt like a coward. He wished that he hadn't repressed his sexuality for all of those years—that he'd had the strength to honor both his own nature and his divine calling. Instead, he'd gone with the program and buried his true identity. He'd sacrificed so many parts of himself to a Church that had discarded him like trash. Those moments with Kirk released feelings that he'd never had before or since, but it had also blown his life into unrecognizable pieces. He thought of the wasted decades. He'd lived a long personal tribulation, wholly isolated and ruined.

The smell of diesel invaded his senses as he disembarked at his stop. A wave of depression filled Calvin on the ride home, and he wanted nothing more than to collapse and sleep it away.

Walking past the old telephone pole, he rammed all of his fingers into the hole he'd dug earlier. The whole hand buried, he grabbed past the decades of glue and paper and ripped outward with violence.

The thickness of the mass startled him as it all fell to the ground like a cinderblock. The faded poster that remained could have been about anything, but at least it wasn't propaganda. His hand was covered with a sticky glaze, and he stared at it and realized what he had just done. *This kind of act is a crime against the state*, he thought. Huffing and puffing as he ran from the scene, Calvin darted down a nearby alley. Panting, he inhaled the smell of stale piss and rotting garbage as he moved forward—the evergreen sparkle of broken glass strewn across the alley.

My God, that felt good. Where did that even come from? he wondered. This might have been the first public manifestation of his deep hate for the state-Church. A rush of excitement and wonder now replaced the depression that had consumed him on the bus. Like an addict introduced to a powerful drug, he prayed that he could just make the feeling last.

Before he could form another thought, the same might that had blown through him as a boy began to pour down, overflowing his entire being. Liquid lightning activated every cell. His legs became weak and his body trembled as he fell to his knees. His face pointed up, and with the same courage that Calvin had had as a child, he opened his eyes. A tear gashed across the sky as far as he could see, and at the center, the same light that he'd seen as a boy, the very same image moving closer. A mighty cloud of witnesses fanned out on either side, chanting a chorus in an unknown tongue.

Then a voice so evident in his heart that he didn't need an acoustic version: "I have put my words in your mouth."

"But who am I?" Calvin responded. "I've lost my calling, I'm bitter, I'm ga—"

"My grace is sufficient for you. My power is made perfect in your weakness."

He closed his eyes, remembering that God had always spoken this way to him, with words from Scripture.

Hours seemed to pass in God's presence, but in actual time, only moments passed. Calvin opened his eyes, still kneeling on the cracked concrete, and saw everything back in its place. His legs were jittery, still feeling the glory in every fiber of his skin, bones, and spirit.

"I feel it...finally, I can feel it again," he said.

Chapter Four

Calvin walked to his small apartment. When he entered, he went into his barren bedroom and stared at the closet, debating whether to go inside. Imbued with a new boldness to confront his past head-on, he went in and pulled down the box. He'd thought many times about destroying its contents, but something had always stopped him. His old journal, photos, and a red scrapbook from his ministry days were still buried there. He had shoved his painful memories deep inside for a long time, and likewise, he'd entombed this physical evidence.

When he dusted off the red cover and paged through it, he saw recognition awards, a copy of his college diploma, and the official letter credentialing him as a minister. There was a program from a national youth convention with his name listed as a keynote speaker. It struck him to see the sudden end of things just past the middle—blank pages that he'd always intended to fill while still a young man.

He laid the scrapbook on his bed and pulled out the scattered pictures. He rifled through them, reliving moments with a smile, but stopped on one with a sick feeling in his stomach.

Calvin pictured together with Kirk, the children's minister at the church. Their arms were draped around each other, Kirk flashing that dimpled smile that made everything seem alright. They'd been inseparable in those early days, working at the church. He'd found himself infatuated with a few male friends over the decades, but Kirk was the first one he'd loved with his whole heart—true love he'd never experienced before or since. Short but explosive. Haunting and life-altering.

He took a pen from his uniform pocket and opened the old journal to the first blank page. Calvin wrote with such intensity that his words, like flames, consumed the pages. He'd documented his wandering, isolation, and struggles for the last twenty years, writing about his vision and renewed calling. He wrote about how he had finally battled the demons that this very journal represented to him.

"Maybe I was never meant for conventional ministry," Calvin wrote.

Pausing for a moment, he felt a new revelation descend down and absorb into his mind. He pressed his pen deeper into the page and continued to pour inspiration out in ink.

"If I stayed in the Church, if I lived the lie, I would be a part of this abomination today. My extended pain, my unrelenting heartbreak, may be my salvation."

"Is it possible that all of my past prepared me for this exact moment?"

"God put a message in my heart, and I will speak it to the world. Today!"

Still experiencing spiritual ecstasy, he felt divinely led to put God's message out through a livestream video.

He drafted a three-point outline, trusting that he would be given all of the right words.

1. Invitation to the oppressed, the poor, the stranger, those cast aside by the Church.

2. Appeal to genuine believers that have been misled. Return to your "First Love."

3. A harsh rebuke to Church leaders that prioritize political power over all else.

He continued to write, "They threw me out, ruined my life, and declared me an apostate. But an apostate is someone who abandons their faith. I never did, even in my worst moments. This so-called Church, on the other hand, long-ago turned away from the true faith."

Chapter Five

Calvin sat on the worn sofa, studying the tripod that he'd retrofitted to hold his phone. He hoped that the tape would hold during the live stream, and feared that the phone might fall and send a live feed of his carpet matted with years of spilled Mountain Dew.

He trembled with nervousness. He had cloistered himself for decades and only seen other people on TV, on the bus, or when he went to the grocery store. Doing this video went against every impulse that he'd programmed into himself for all these years. But still, he knew that it must happen.

He checked the camera-view of the phone and noticed the darkness in his living room. He went to the blinds and saw years, maybe decades of dust that had been layered there. He opened them just enough to bring in light, but not so much that someone could see inside. The dust particles he set free streamed into his nose, circulated through his respiratory system, and he coughed them back out violently.

Calvin walked around the room, psyching himself up, then caught a glimpse of his reflection in the darkened TV screen. He could see his flabby, rounded frame, his too-large untucked shirt, and the outdated glasses on his face.

"I can't do it, I can't do it, I just can't do it!"

He fell back onto the sofa, the rate of his breathing increasing, his chest tightening. For a moment, he thought that it might be a heart attack or something worse.

At the peak of his panic, he began to hear a familiar, still-small voice repeating simple words of comfort:

"Be still. Be still. Be still."

Even in his current state of mind, he recognized the words from the Book of Psalms. "Be still and know that I am God."

Indeed, he could feel the growing blanket of comfort in those words. He could feel his pulse slowing, his breath normalizing, and the tension in his chest eased.

The anxiety did not leave Calvin's mind, but it did start to reverse. And at that moment, he committed a flagrant act of faith. He hit 'record.'

His vocal cords began to engage, and with the very first intonations, his apprehensions and fears melted away. Calvin started delivering his first sermon in over twenty years. The most important sermon of his entire life.

Calvin basked in the euphoria that he'd always felt after delivering a sermon that he knew connected, piercing through to the soul. Calvin wanted to celebrate. He wanted to give thanks for this miracle. He grabbed his favorite gospel cassette, blasted it, danced, clapped, and shouted all around his small apartment.

Curiosity drove him to check his livestream's statistics, and it astonished him to see almost 10,000 views.

He wondered how it could be possible from a new account with zero following.

Not very familiar with the platform, it took him a while to notice the comments. He couldn't help himself and began reading the barbaric attacks.

The Church's international troll army and government bots must be engaged already, he thought. He refreshed the page minutes later and found the video disabled, but the nasty comments kept piling up. Impulse drove him to continue refreshing, but he started to notice something different: Hundreds of new comments carried the same message.

"We are with you, brother!"

Embedded in every supportive message, a link to new individual pages with the full video still available.

"My God!" Calvin shouted.

It was a coordinated effort to thwart censors, battle trolls, and amplify his message.

"There's a resistance!"

Calvin was exhausted in every way, but he couldn't stop looking at his original video's comments.

The video itself continued to spread like a virus throughout the internet. The government technicians and Church censors couldn't keep up. They couldn't stop the message.

Comments, now totaling over 1,000, he saw something new and terrifying. The trolls had now started calling him out by name.

"They've identified me now," he said, his voice shaking.

He'd expected it at some point, but it still gave him pause. He assumed that they might already know his physical location. He could feel in his guts that the stakes had risen.

Stories in the media started popping up, dismissing him as a depraved sodomite, disgruntled because of his termination from the Church. Others focused on his status as a nobody, decades of dead-end jobs, and bankruptcies. He thought that the rapid pace of propaganda couldn't get worse until he saw an interview on the Church's TV network. Kirk's piercing blue eyes now looked dead as he stared into the cameras. He had a new and disturbing nervous tic, squinting his eyes as if absorbing pain.

Calvin could see how they'd purged all of the life from him, and he mourned for Kirk. The person that had changed his world no longer existed.

He read a script accusing Calvin of sexually assaulting him when they'd worked together. He went on to make even more monstrous claims, lying to the entire world. Calvin's pain rolled through him like a storm. The old wounds that he thought he'd conquered started to throb.

He looked at his email and saw that he had over 1,000 new messages. He read many death threats and some disingenuous invitations for him to defend himself on Church-controlled media.

Then he saw a grouping of emails, all with the same subject line: "Fighting the good fight!"

Calvin started reading the supportive emails, and they all listed different ways that the resistance was helping his cause. One email contained a link to a story posted on the Patriot & Prophet website. The defamatory content was replaced with his full video message. He clicked another link for the Church's TV network, but discovered that the resistance had hacked it, taking it down. Supportive comments stood in the place of the vile attacks all over the internet.

He witnessed such a sophisticated effort in real-time. *It must be a large group of people all over the world*, he thought.

As he daydreamed about everything happening behind the scenes, the sound of his phone startled him. He just stared as it kept ringing.

He wondered if he should answer. He thought that it could be a death threat, or it could be the resistance.

"Or it could just be a wrong number."

He realized that they couldn't do much more to him, so he answered.

"Hello."

"Brother, there is not much time, so please just let me speak a word of knowledge to you." The women spoke in a Southern-accented baritone.

"OK," Calvin responded.

"I am Anna the Prophet, and you should know that righteous men and women all over this world are fighting for you."

"I've seen that on—"

"Brother, please listen. You've planted seeds today, prophets have been called, and heroes of the true faith have been born. No matter what happens next, God wants you to know these truths."

"Th—thank you for that," Calvin whispered.

"Now, Brother, I know that you don't know me, but we have special brothers and sisters coming to your home ri—"

"You know where I li—"

"Brother Calvin, time is short. Gather whatever you must and get ready. Those serving the Whore of Babylon will arrest you, so we want to move you underground."

"Where am I go—"

"Lord bless and keep you, Brother. Get ready!" the prophet said, and she disconnected the call.

Calvin grabbed a garbage bag and threw in things that he might need: his prized Walkman, a dozen cassettes, and a few days' worth of clothes. He paced the apartment, having second thoughts about what he should do next.

Should I just run off on my own? How do I know Prophet Anna is for real?

He wondered if he shouldn't run at all—if maybe he should stay right there and let the morality officers take him away, just like they'd done to that young man in the store.

"I'm no better than him," he said aloud.

Calvin stacked his scrapbook, pictures, and journal and sat on the sofa. He reflected for a moment, and then it came to him.

He already existed in a different world, on a different spiritual plane. His faith finally smoldered again inside him.

"They can't extinguish it, no matter what happens next."

Acknowledgments

A book is never a solo endeavor, and I have many people to thank for helping bring *Apostate* to light. My deepest gratitude to the team at *A Thin Slice of Anxiety* for first believing in this story and giving it a home. Thank you to the insightful instructors and fellow writers at Gotham Writers Workshop, whose early feedback was invaluable.

For this edition, a special thank you to my cover designer, Rafal Kucharczuk, for capturing the story's soul in a single image, and to my editor, Lillian Boyd, for her keen eye and insightful guidance on the text.

On a personal note, none of this would be possible without the unwavering support and encouragement of my husband, who is my constant source of strength and inspiration. My thanks also go to my family and friends, who have cheered me on throughout this journey. And to my wonderful #BookTok followers, your enthusiasm and encouragement are a constant boost to my spirits.

And finally, to you, the reader. Thank you for taking a chance on this story and stepping into Calvin's world. You are the reason I write.

Enjoy the Story? The Journey Continues...

Thank you for reading *Apostate: The First Heresy*. If you're wondering what happens next to Calvin, the best way to find out is by joining my reader community.

As a subscriber, you will be the first to know when *Part Two* is released, get exclusive behind-the-scenes content, and receive updates on my other novels.

Join the community by signing up for my newsletter and never miss a story:

www.cjloveman.com

Coming Soon from C.J. Loveman...

His duty was to Rome. His heart belonged to his Jewish servant.

For Centurion Gaius Julius Vigilis, life in Roman-occupied Galilee is one of brutal discipline and order. But when a mysterious rabbi performs an undeniable miracle, healing his beloved Tobias, the foundations of Gaius's world are shattered.

Targeted by his ruthless superior, Tribune Valerius, Gaius is plunged into a perilous game of political intrigue where every loyalty is tested. With his career, his honor, and the life of the man he loves on the line, Gaius must discover that true strength is not found in the might of a legion, but in the courage to embrace a love that is treason and a faith that is rebellion.

About the Author

C.J. Loveman crafts historical and dystopian tales about characters caught at the crossroads of faith, identity, and rebellion. He is the author of the *Apostate* series and the forthcoming novel, *The Centurion's Embrace*. His unique perspective was forged in the crucible of an evangelical Bible college, where his training to become a minister collided with a profound struggle over his own identity. That conflict between belief and self-discovery set him on a new course, and now it fuels his stories of outcasts, rebels, and seekers.

I've always been fascinated by the moments where a single decision changes everything. For me, that moment came while I was studying to be an evangelical minister, a path I felt called to until my own identity came into direct conflict with the rigid teachings about my deeply held faith.

Navigating that struggle and the wounds that came with it now fuels my writing. I love to explore the stories of outcasts, rebels, and seekers who are forced to question the world around them. Whether it's in a reimagined past or a dark near-future, my goal is to put you right there in the heart of their struggle and their hope.

If you have ever felt like an outcast, even in your own life, I want to create a place for you. I am writing for you.

As an older dad with young kids, life is beautifully chaotic. When I'm not writing, my husband and I are usually chasing after our children, traveling when we get the chance, or enjoying a peaceful walk with our dog. Thanks for stopping by!